This book belongs to:

Dedication:
For our son, Kieran Joseph
Dan & Rhonda Vallely

THE GREAT POSSUM CREEK BUSH FIRE

Poem by Dan Vallely
Pictures by Yvonne Perrin

NATIONAL

BAKERY

It was a sleepy Sunday morning
Just a little after dawning
And the town of Possum Creek was calm and still.
As the animals were stirring
A disaster was occurring
As a flame burst forth upon a distant hill.

Big Red Kangaroo on rising
Thought it quite surprising
That the smell of smoke lay heavy on the air.
For the council of the shire
Had placed a total ban on fire
And they'd all been warned to take the utmost care.

As he ran into the clearing
The event that he'd been fearing
Was an awful fact, as he could plainly tell.
For a wall of flames was burning
And was very quickly turning
All the bush to ashes, just near Wombats' Well.

It was clear Big Red was worried
As with frantic haste he scurried
To the firehouse to set off the alarm.
Within seconds bells were ringing,
And the firetruck was bringing
All the volunteers to fight for Wombats' farm.

Peter Possum did the driving
And they saw upon arriving
That the flames had very nearly won the day.
They were licking round the stable
And the youngest wombat, Mabel,
Was leading all the horses far away.

The fire chief was Ed Galah,
Who drove an extra special car
Whose klaxon guaranteed to wake the dead,
As he drove up, klaxon blaring,
Very dignified of bearing,
They'd already lost the fodder storage shed.

Ed Galah, with cool precision,
Made his vital first decision
As he put the dingo brothers on the pumps.
Two numbats manned the hoses
And demolished several roses
And a beehive, causing many painful lumps.

By the time their aim was better
There was nothing any wetter
Than the volunteers, a sorry dripping bunch.
But their spirit was unbroken,
No faint-hearted words were spoken
Even though they hadn't time to stop for lunch.

Slowly they were winning
For the ranks of flames were thinning
And finally the house was safe at last.
But the clean-up was aborted
When a sharp-eyed crow reported
That the flames on Possum Creek were closing fast.

So with bells a-madly clanging
And equipment all a-banging
They sped back to town to start the fight anew.
From atop the fire station
They then gazed with consternation
On the blackened fields where corn and wheat once grew.

Tom Echidna, who was mayor,
Ever keen to do his share
Displayed to all his loyalty and grit.
With a flourish brave and bold,
He threw off his chain of gold
And proudly marched away to do his bit.

As the ring of flames came closer,
Billy Platypus, the grocer,
Shouted, "Men, although the water's running low,
Because of next week's picnic races
I've bought fifty dozen cases
Of the finest lemonade, as you all know.

"And if vigorously shaken
Unless I'm much mistaken,
As extinguishers they'll really fit the bill."
And so with scant decorum
They raced back to Billy's store-room
That lay behind the old abandoned mill.

FINEST
LEMON

They stood, bottles at the ready,
As the fire chief said "Steady",
With courage rare they made their final stand.
And though the blaze approached them
And very nearly poached them
The bushland heroes kept it well in hand.

BEST
ADE

By the time that they were finished
The flames were quite diminished
And relief was plain on every face in town.
Twelve hours, they had fought it
And as sure as I report it
With exhaustion every creature then fell down.

FINEST
LEMONADE

Now if you ever spend a week
Down there with friends at Possum Creek
The locals will be happy to relate
How as the flames were leaping higher
They bravely soda-popped the fire
And in the end just beat it by a crate.

Published by National Book Distributors
19A Roger Street, Brookvale NSW 2100 Australia
First Edition 1988
Paperback Edition 1989
Reprinted 1989, 1990 (3 times), 1991

Printed in Hong Kong by Everbest Printing Co. Ltd
National Library of Australia Cataloguing-in-Publication data
ISBN 1 875580 17 4